The
Crocodile
in the
Tree

THIS IS A BORZOI BOOK PUBLISHED BY ALFRED A. KNOPF, INC.

Copyright © 1973 by Roger Duvoisin

All rights reserved under International and Pan-American Copyright Conventions. Published in the United States by Alfred A. Knopf, Inc., New York. Distributed by Random House, Inc., New York. Originally published in Great Britain by the Bodley Head, Ltd.

Library of Congress Cataloging in Publication Data

Duvoisin, Roger Antoine   The crocodile in the tree.
SUMMARY: A crocodile befriended by the barnyard animals tries to prove to the farmer's wife that he can be her friend too. I. Title.
PZ7.D957Cr   [E]   72-5270 ISBN 0-394-82516-0   ISBN 0-394-92516-5 (lib. bdg.)

Manufactured in the United States of America

The Crocodile in the Tree

Roger Duvoisin

Alfred A. Knopf · New York

Bertha the duck and Johnny the rabbit were sitting under the old oak tree when Johnny cried, "Bertha! Up there! I just saw a crocodile's tail sticking out of that hole in the trunk!"

"Don't worry, Johnny, we all imagine things at times."

"I said *I saw a crocodile's tail*," cried Johnny, "and I will not stay here another moment. Good-bye."

"Good morning, Bertha," said a voice behind the duck.

Bertha spun around and came face to face with a crocodile's head.

"Please, Bertha," said the crocodile's head, "stay a while so we can talk a bit. Don't be afraid. I wouldn't think of eating you up."

The crocodile's head opened its long, long mouth in a smile which showed four long, long rows of teeth.

"What are you?" asked Bertha, "A crocodile or just a crocodile's head?"

"A whole crocodile," answered the crocodile's head. "The rest of me is up there inside the trunk. Not comfortable, I dare say!"

"Where do you come from?" asked Bertha.

"That's not important. I am here, and that's what counts. I stay in this hollow tree during the day. At night I go out to stretch on the grass, look at the moon, and swim in the pond. I do miss the sun. Can you imagine a crocodile who can't doze in the sun? My color will soon fade and I will look like an unripe apple. And, oh, I do miss flowers so!"

"Then why do you hide in that tree?"

"I must. Everyone is afraid of crocodiles because of their many teeth. If your farmer saw me he might take his gun and, BOOM, that would be the end of me. Wouldn't that be sad? After all, I still have a good four hundred years to live. People should know that there are good crocodiles."

"Then I won't leave you here," said Bertha. "I'll hide you in the barn where you will not have to keep your tail up all day. And don't be afraid of Mr. Sweetpeas, the farmer. He and his wife have gone to the market. Come, I will introduce you to the barnyard."

What a commotion the animals made when they saw the crocodile. The horses and the cows reared and kicked. The sheep and the pig ran under the chicken house. The goat jumped onto the tractor. The hens and the ducks flew to the top of the barn with the pigeons. And Coco the dog barked until he was hoarse.

"You see what I mean," moaned the crocodile. "I frighten them all and I'm not even showing my teeth."

"Stop barking," said Bertha to Coco.

"A dog *must* bark," answered Coco. "If I didn't bark who would?"

Finally Coco smelled the crocodile all over and said he was all right. Then he went to chew on an old bone.

Seeing this, all the animals stopped kicking, shrieking, crowing, and bleating and came to look at the crocodile.

"My friend will live with us," explained Bertha. "You will love him for he is kind and only uses his teeth for smiling."

"That's all very well," said Carrot the cat. "*I* like him, but what about Mr. and Mrs. Sweetpeas?"

"We will hide my crocodile in the barn until we can show Mr. Sweetpeas that he is a *good* crocodile," said Bertha.

Everyone worked so hard to hide the crocodile in straw that he was moved to tears.

"Believe me, my friends, these are *good* crocodile's tears," he said.

Bertha was like a mother to her crocodile. She fed him, she tucked him in at night, and she warned him when the farmer or his wife came to the barnyard so he could slip under the hay.

All went well until, one day, Mrs. Sweetpeas burst into the barn to fetch some apples while Bertha and Coco were chatting with the crocodile. Coco barely had time to pull some hay over the crocodile and Bertha to sit on his head with her wings spread out.

"What are you doing here, Bertha?" asked Mrs. Sweetpeas. "Laying eggs where you shouldn't? Let me see."

She pushed Bertha aside and saw the crocodile's head!

"Oh, hello," said the crocodile with his sweetest smile.

"*A crocodile! A crocodile!*" screamed Mrs. Sweetpeas and she ran out of the barn to the farmhouse.

"There is a crocodile in the barn and the duck was sitting on its head!" she cried out to Mr. Sweetpeas.

"What are you saying?" asked her husband.

"I said Bertha was sitting on a crocodile's head!"

"Are you out of your mind, dear?"

"I know what I see and I *saw* Bertha sitting on a crocodile's head. Go and see for yourself. That is, if you are not afraid of crocodiles."

So, Mr. Sweetpeas went to look.

In the meantime, the animals in the barn worried about their crocodile.

"The police will come," said Bertha, "and they will take our crocodile to the zoo."

"Or kill it," said Carrot the cat.

"I have an idea," said Coco. "There is a big loose board behind the pile of hay in the barn, and I'm the only one who knows where it is. I found it one day as I was running after a rat. That's where I hide my bones. Fine place to hide a crocodile."

So the crocodile slipped under the board while Coco covered it with hay.

"Watch out!" cried Bertha. "Here comes Mr. Sweetpeas. Everyone try to look busy and innocent."

Mr. Sweetpeas looked around and behind and under everything in the barnyard but there was no crocodile. He called Coco.

"Come, Coco, smell the crocodile!"

Coco wagged his tail and ran everywhere, barking loudly. Then he went to sleep in his kennel as if he couldn't care less about crocodiles.

"I knew there was no crocodile," said Mr. Sweetpeas. "I wonder what has come over Marguerite." And he returned to the farmhouse.

All the animals were full of joy. All except the crocodile. He looked sad when he came out from under the barn floor.

"The farmer's wife," he sighed. "She seems like such a sweet lady. I am so sad that I have scared her. I already like her very much."

"She is nice," said Carrot. "She loves us so much and takes such good care of us."

"And how she loves flowers," added Bertha. "Most of the day we see her bending down over her flower beds, picking out weeds and planting new flowers. Her garden is beautiful."

"I adore flowers, too," sighed the crocodile. "The farmer's wife and I could be such good friends. We have so much in common!"

That night the crocodile thought about the good farmer's wife and he said to himself, "If I could only let her know how much I like her!"

All of a sudden, he smiled with all his teeth. Now he knew what to do.

At dawn, before the farmers were up, he went to the meadow to pick a beautiful bouquet of white daisies mixed with lovely wild grasses. He took it to the farmhouse porch and placed it on the little table where Mrs. Sweetpeas served breakfast on sunny days.

Mrs. Sweetpeas was delighted when she saw the bouquet.

"Oh, darling," she said to her husband, "it was so nice and thoughtful of you to pick these daisies for me."

"I did not pick them," said Mr. Sweetpeas.

"Then who did?" she wondered.

The next morning the crocodile brought a big bunch of bergamots set among wild ferns.

Then the morning after that, the crocodile made a bouquet of brown-eyed Susans, which he picked at the edge of the woods.

Then it was a bouquet of tall loosestrifes which grew beyond the pond. Their purple colors were as fresh as the morning sky.

Mrs. Sweetpeas grew happier each morning at the sight of these lovely flowers. But she could not guess who had picked them.

"We must find out who brings these bouquets for you," declared Mr. Sweetpeas.

Before dawn, the following morning Mr. and Mrs. Sweetpeas went down to the living room to watch from behind the porch door. Shortly after, the crocodile appeared with a brilliant bouquet of the wild cardinal flowers which grew beside the stream.

"Well," exclaimed the farmer. "So there *was* a crocodile in the barn after all! And, my dear, what a considerate crocodile!"

"Such a darling crocodile," exclaimed Mrs. Sweetpeas. "He is an artist with flowers and he loves them as much as I do."

She ran to the crocodile to pat him and to thank him for all the lovely bouquets while Mr. Sweetpeas shook his paw.

All the animals on the farm, led by Bertha, Coco, and Carrot, came running to join in the rejoicing.

From then on there were three to care for the farm flower garden:
Mrs. Sweetpeas, the crocodile, and Bertha. Never again did the crocodile have to hide under the barn floor or in the tree.

"Life is so beautiful when we have so much in common with a friend,"
mused the crocodile.